L·U·C·Y
and the
Magic
Loom

L·U·C·Y
and the
Magic
Loom

A
Rainbow Loomer's
Adventure Story

by Alice Downes

SKY PONY PRESS
NEW YORK

Copyright © 2015 by Hollan Publishing, Inc.

Sky Pony Press books may be purchased in bulk at special discounts for sales promotion, corporate gifts, fund-raising, or educational purposes. Special editions can also be created to specifications. For details, contact the Special Sales Department, Sky Pony Press, 307 West 36th Street, 11th Floor, New York, NY 10018 or info@skyhorsepublishing.com.

Sky Pony® is a registered trademark of Skyhorse Publishing, Inc.®, a Delaware corporation.

Visit our website at www.skyponypress.com.

10 9 8 7 6 5 4 3 2 1

Library of Congress Cataloging-in-Publication Data

Downes, Alice.
  Lucy and the magic loom / Alice Downes.
     pages cm. -- (A rainbow loomer's adventure story ; 1)
  Summary: "Meet Lucy--twelve years old, missing her best friend, and just waiting for an adventure to come her way. When she discovers a golden magic loom, it leads her into an enchanted world"-- Provided by publisher.
  ISBN 978-1-63450-137-8 (paperback)
  [1. Magic--Fiction. 2. Friendship--Fiction. 3. Adventure and adventurers--Fiction.] I. Title.
  PZ7.D75767Ls 2015
  [Fic]--dc23
2015001027

Cover design and illustration by Jan Gerardi

Ebook ISBN: 978-1-63450-891-9

Printed in Canada

Chapter One

It was raining. Twelve-year-old Lucy Stillwater-Smith was sitting at her favorite window seat on the second floor of 163 Terrier Square, writing a letter to her best friend. Alyssa Jones had moved to America in July. It was November now, and Lucy missed her best friend every minute of the day. But rainy, dark, damp Saturday afternoons were the absolute worst. The girls texted each other at least ten times a day during the week, and spoke on the phone every Tuesday night. On the day Alyssa left, the girls swore they would exchange letters every Saturday, and, so far, they'd kept their promise.

Dear Alyssa,

I miss you horribly. I really, really do. It has rained every day in London since the first of November—it feels damp all the time! Everyone at Saint Chester's sends love and kisses—even Mrs. Cheeks the librarian asked about you this week. Meanie Sondra White asked me for your address in New York. Can you believe it? I told her I'd lost it. LOL! I will write again just as soon as something interesting happens here— not! You would never hear from me again if I did that! I plan on enjoying a strawberry and banana smoothie this afternoon in honor of your favorite colors—pink and yellow. My favorite color remains lavender, just so you know. The Doctors continue to work all the time. If I ever see them again in the flesh, I'm sure they would send you greetings. Ha! Ha! Ha! Did you like the glow-in-the-dark Rainbow Loom bracelet I sent you last week? I thought it was awesome— just like you. I LOVED the pink and purple headband you made me. Really!

*It doesn't look nearly as silly as you
worried it might.
Your true best friend forever,
Lucy Stillwater-Smith*

Lucy put down her purple gel pen and stared out the window to the park across the street. The little tea shop was closed because of the rain, and her friendly neighbor, old Mrs. Gloucester, who could usually be found in the park walking her dog, Mr. Poppins, this time of day, was nowhere to be seen. The windows of the two hundred-year-old white stone town house in which Lucy sat seemed to shake with the harsh November wind. "Maybe the ghosts miss Alyssa as well," Lucy said out loud, turning from the window to peer expectantly around the empty room. She waited for a response, holding her breath, but nothing happened. "Nothing interesting ever happens here," Lucy sighed, suddenly exasperated and lonely. She missed Alyssa so much her stomach hurt. Lucy turned back to the window.

"The Doctors" were Lucy's parents. Her father was the Stillwater in Lucy's last name, and her mother was the Smith. Lucy's mother looked after children with cancer and Lucy's father was attempting to cure a collection of terrifying infectious diseases with scary-sounding names. The Doctors were very, very, very, very busy. They left the town house on the square together before the sun came up every morning and rode their bicycles to the hospital. They came home long after Lucy was in bed, even on weekends. The Doctors communicated with their daughter via note: they left little sticky note missives on the kitchen counter, on Lucy's toothbrush, or on the milk jug in the fridge. Sometimes her father hid notes in the pages of the books Lucy read. It was all very sweet, but if truth be told, Lucy was over the notes. She missed hanging out with her parents. She'd trade all of their cute messages for one lazy Sunday afternoon of family time.

Miss Abigail Sanders had minded Lucy since before time began. White-haired, twinkly-eyed, with massive, jiggly arms, Abigail smelled like a freshly baked cake and her laugh sounded like Christmas bells. Lucy didn't need "minding" anymore, but she was glad to have Abigail's company — Lucy loved her more than chocolate and summer holidays put together.

Besides keeping Lucy company, Abigail was also responsible for ensuring the

Stillwater-Smith family had everything they needed to survive: endless tins of green tea, tea biscuits, bananas, strawberries, school supplies and Rainbow Loom elastics for Lucy, Wi-Fi, freshly plumped-up bicycle tires, and bottles of water and clean gym shorts so Dr. Stillwater could go running on Tuesdays and Thursdays, and the same for Dr. Smith, who practiced hot yoga on Mondays and Wednesdays. Lucy didn't like to run or do hot yoga. Abigail and Lucy liked to eat tea biscuits or grapes in the kitchen most afternoons after school and read. The two of them were awed by the discipline of Lucy's parents—their dedication was impressive, but it was also massively boring at times. And nothing ever changed.

As much as her parents loved exercise and spending time at the hospital, Lucy loved creating beautiful things. Before Alyssa moved, Lucy made her a collage. She printed pictures from her camera and the Internet, of the people and places Alyssa loved most—Poppins the dog, Lucy, the table in the Stillwater-Smith kitchen. Next, she painted the background blue—to represent the ocean. When it dried, she created a collage bridge between London and New York and added the pictures she printed. Abigail had it framed at the shop on High Street. Alyssa cried when Lucy gave it to her. A few days later, Lucy's mum left a note in her lunch bag, signed with extra hugs and kisses, asking Lucy to consider creating pictures for the rooms of her sick patients. Instead, Lucy came up with the idea of making double-width Rainbow Loom friendship bracelets. Her mother was delighted.

Maybe *that's* what she would do for the rest of this rainy afternoon! Lucy's mum always said the best thing to do when you feel lonely is be kind to someone else. Before she got started, Lucy took one more look out the window—just to make sure it was still raining, and that's when she saw it.

On the town house stoop far below—and just visible from her window perch—Lucy saw a large package, intricately wrapped with green string and gray duct tape, resting against the front door of the town house, just out of the rain. She jumped from her seat and flew down the two flights of stairs to the front door—it had to be a surprise from Alyssa! What else could it be?

"What's going on out there?" Abigail called from the kitchen. "Don't make such a racket,

Lucy. You'll cause my cake to fall and ruin our tea."

"I'll explain in a minute, Abigail," Lucy laughed as she slid across the entry hall floor and threw open the front door.

The package on the front step was huge—two feet by two feet—and covered in brown recycled paper that seemed to glow with a soft lavender color. Lucy had the strange sensation of knowing without a doubt that whatever was inside the package was important and beautiful and hers. She leaned down to pick it up with both hands. Just then, a powerful wet gust of wind wrapped itself around the package and Lucy, sending them both tumbling backward into the front hall. The front door slammed shut and Lucy found herself eye-to-eye with the address label on the box. Strangely, the package wasn't the least bit wet.

The lettering on the address label was written by hand, wonderfully pretty, and sparkled in a glittering rainbow of bright primary colors. Lucy stared at it. She blinked. How was it possible? The package wasn't for her! This stunning bit of information was a physical shock, as sharp and startling as if someone had tugged on her ponytail. The label read:

Miss Sallee Ratchford-Jones III
163 and ½ Terrier Square
London
United Kingdom
The World
INCREDIBLY FRAGILE

Lucy, the Doctors, and Abigail lived at 163 Terrier Square, not 163 and ½ Terrier Square. Addresses didn't come in halves! Everybody knew that.

Suddenly Lucy was overcome with a tidal wave of sadness—if Alyssa still lived around the corner, Lucy would throw on her purple rain slicker, grab her yellow umbrella and the box, and run to Alyssa's house to discuss their options. Together the girls would make a list of possible solutions and pick their favorite. They would settle on the details of a complete plan—including what to wear and who to share the secret with—after they ate their afternoon rainy-day cake and tea.

But Alyssa wasn't around the corner anymore. Lucy's phone was out of juice (and charging upstairs on the second floor). The Doctors weren't home (surprise, surprise), and

Abigail was distracted in the kitchen. The package Lucy was nose-to-nose with on the marble floor was clearly meant for her—Lucy could feel this deep down in her bones—but it was addressed to someone else.

Lucy closed her eyes and pictured Alyssa's serious and trustworthy face. She could almost hear Alyssa saying what she always said: "Trust your instincts, Lucy. I have never known your instincts to be anything but spot-on." Lucy kept her eyes closed and began to count backward from fifty. Abigail had taught Lucy to do this when she was little—if you had a perfect idea but you weren't sure if it was the *best* idea, distract yourself by counting backward from fifty. If, when you were done, your perfect idea was still there, at the front and center of your brain, it was possible it *was* a good idea after all. Next, you were supposed to ask someone else their opinion of your good idea.

Lucy thought about it. She still wasn't quite sure, and clearly there was no one around to ask. She took a deep breath and counted backward from ten just to be extra, extra sure she wanted to do what she was planning to do. Then, with a secret little squeal, she tugged the string that held the wrapping on the package together.

"My goodness, Lucy. What in heaven's name do you have on your lap?" Lucy's mum danced through the front door, shaking the rain off her umbrella. She stopped in her tracks and smiled at her daughter, who was sitting on the rain-damp floor with the massive box in her lap, about to tug open the string and the wrapping. Lucy stopped, shocked into stillness: the Doctors never came home in the afternoon. Abigail came running in from the kitchen, wringing her hands together and speaking in that high singsong voice she only ever used when she was discombobulated.

"Oh, dear me. Is something wrong, Dr. Smith? What are you doing home at this hour?"

"What do you have there, Lucy?" her mum asked again. She kissed Abigail's cheek absent-mindedly. "I forgot my phone," she said, reaching down to pluck the box out of Lucy's lap without taking off her raincoat. The box was so big and the hallway floor was so slippery from the rain and wind, Lucy's mum almost fell backward. Abigail reached out to help her, but she managed to steady herself. With her one spare hand, she dug around in her backpack, found her glasses, and slid them over her nose. She read the label on the box and frowned.

"This box isn't addressed to you, Lucy. You can't open packages that aren't meant for you. What are you thinking?" She sounded cross.

"Where did this package come from, Lucy?" Abigail asked, speaking over Dr. Smith.

"It magically appeared on the landing, long after today's mail came. It feels like it belongs to me," Lucy tried to explain.

"Things don't *feel* like they belong to you Lucy—they do or they don't. This is clearly someone else's property," said her mum.

"But it's almost as if it likes me."

"Things don't have feelings, Lucy, obviously. What is wrong with you?"

"Mum, I know it sounds crazy, but I am positive this package belongs to me."

"Lucy, I am disappointed in you. You can't have everything you want all the time. Whomever this box belongs to is expecting it. You should know better. I am taking it up to my office until we figure this out. I think you should spend the rest of the afternoon in your room—no phone, no games, no TV—don't make that face, my beautiful girl! What you were about to do was *steal*. I'm serious. I want you to spend the afternoon thinking about that."

Lucy's mum turned on her heels and began climbing the stairs, cradling the box between her arms. She didn't look back.

Lucy felt like she was going to cry.

"You better do as she says, luv," Abigail whispered. "Go on with you. She's right, you know. But don't worry, I will sneak you some tea just as soon as I can."

Chapter Two

Lucy's bedroom was located on the second floor of 163 Terrier Square. She had a bed with a soft purple bedspread and a walk-in closet where she sometimes liked to read. In one corner there was a built-in bookcase jam-packed with Lucy's favorite books. A few dusty old tomes from her mother's childhood lived on the top shelf. Lucy kept them only because it pleased her mum—she hadn't actually read them yet.

In the opposite corner from Lucy's bookcase, between the window and the window seat that looked out over the park, was more pretty built-in shelving. This was where Lucy kept her trinkets and treasures, including the dolls she loved when she was little and couldn't part with. It's there where she displayed pictures of Alyssa and other friends, mementoes from family trips, and her collection of cute fuzzy animal plush toys. Her treasured musical jewelry box lived on the second shelf, along her games and her neatly color-coded boxes of craft supplies—including the Rainbow Loom she loved so much.

Lucy's room was directly below the Doctors' shared home office on the third floor. Lucy wasn't allowed to go into their office without permission. Even Abigail needed to ask for an OK before stepping in to dust.

The clock struck two and then the town house was quiet. The silence was broken for a moment by the sound of Lucy's mum flying down the stairs and charging out the front door into the rain. She didn't even pop her head in to say goodbye—clearly, she was still upset. Lucy absentmindedly picked at the little balls of fluff on her favorite pink sweater. She had changed with the hope that the pink softness would make her feel better. It didn't. With nothing to distract her, all she could think about was the package upstairs in her mother's office. Where had it come from? Who was it really for? Who was the mysterious girl it was addressed to?

Lucy was lying on her back on the bed, splayed on top of her comforter. She flipped onto her stomach and counted backward from one hundred. Next, she flipped dramatically onto her back and counted forward to two hundred. She did this four more times until she couldn't stand it anymore—sometimes a girl had to do what a girl had to do! In a flash, Lucy was on her feet, out the door of her room and up the stairs.

Abigail typically took a long nap in the afternoon. Luckily, once the older woman was down and asleep, nothing could wake her. Lucy figured she had a good solid hour before Abigail was up here with an afternoon snack and a cup of tea on a silver tray.

Lucy's mother hadn't tried to hide the package. It was sitting on the top of her desk—Lucy spotted it as soon as she opened the door. She felt its odd magical quality immediately, even from across the room. Filled with courage and vim just a few seconds ago, Lucy was momentarily shaken. By nature, Lucy wasn't a rule breaker. Alyssa was the one more inclined to poke around in her parents' closets looking for Christmas treats and birthday presents. Lucy rather liked being surprised and, as a result, didn't go out of her way to spoil the fun. Sneaking about this way wasn't like her. Nevertheless, something was calling her to action.

Slowly and carefully, Lucy walked to the desk. She held the green string again, exactly as she had when her mother arrived home just over an hour ago. This time, the packaging fell away—the string dissolved, the duct tape vanished, and the brown paper evaporated. All that remained on the desk was the address label and a long, narrow black box made of ebony and mother of pearl. In the cool half-light of the gloomy afternoon, it glistened. Lucy gasped. It was beautiful.

Lucy's hands were trembling. Holding her breath, the way you do before you jump into a cold mountain lake early in the summer, she placed her hands on either side of the box's hinged black lid. Lucy counted to three out loud—*one, two, three*—and opened the box.

The purple aura that Lucy had sensed when she first saw the box exploded around her. Light bounced around the room while Lucy stood there, eyes wide open. It was as if the light and the color had a personality and was very happy to see her, in the same way a puppy greets you at the door. And just like a puppy, the light and motion seemed to exhaust itself after a few minutes and settled down. Lucy looked into the open box.

In the box was a gold loom, much like the Rainbow Loom Lucy had upstairs on her craft shelf, but oddly beautiful. Beside the golden loom was a glass hook. Beneath the loom and the hook were a multitude of clear envelopes, each one filled with sparkling elastic bands and labeled in the same handwriting Lucy had seen on the outside of the package. She reached into the box and gently pulled out the envelopes to examine them more closely. One was labeled *See in the Dark* and another was labeled *Invisible*. Another package was filled with emerald green elastics and labeled *Breathe Under Water*. Yet another was bursting with exquisite turquoise blue bands and the label read *Walk Through Walls*.

Lucy suddenly felt nervous. This entire day had been topsy-turvy. First the package arrived. Then her mother came home in the afternoon. Next, Lucy was unfairly sent to her room, and now she was breaking rules willy-nilly. Quickly and quietly, Lucy crammed the clear packages back into the box and closed the lid.

Lucy had to think. She decided to go back downstairs to her room and make a new plan.

❀ ❀ ❀

Sitting crossed-legged on her bed, Lucy was torn. She didn't know what to do next. She couldn't call Alyssa, because her mother had taken her phone. She thought about heading to Abigail's room over the old coach house and waking her up, but this felt like it should be kept a secret. What if Abigail made her give the loom back to whoever Sallee Ratchford-Jones the Third was.

The more she thought about it, the more it seemed that what needed to happen next was obvious; kittens were meant to be petted, kites were meant to be flown, roller coasters were meant to be rode upside down in! Obviously, a loom needed to make things! Maybe if Lucy snuck back upstairs and began weaving, using only the magnificent collection of elastic bands in the box, the magic loom would reveal its secret to her. She had to try.

Taking two stairs at time, Lucy was quickly back in front of the door to her parents' office. As soon as she crossed the threshold, a gentle humming sound floated toward her from the ebony box. It was happy she was back! How weird was that?

Her parents' office had two desks, a wall of six completely full bookcases, and a window seat, much like the one Lucy had in her room. Lucy picked up the ebony box from her mother's desk and carried it with her to the window seat. She climbed onto the cushions, making herself comfortable, and carefully placed the loom onto the cushion beside her. But when she put it down, the loom seemed to twitch and jerk, almost like an unhappy kitten that doesn't want to sit in your lap. Lucy picked it up again. The loom had a surprising weight and heft in comparison to the Rainbow Looms Lucy and Alyssa had used last summer to make each other glow-in-the-dark friendship bracelets and rings.

Lucy concentrated, trying to remember the friendship ring pattern she once knew so well. Suddenly she smiled and turned to the ebony box. Digging past the bands that sparkled like a treasure chest of precious jewels, she found an envelope with the label *Practice*.

"That's exactly what I want to do!" Lucy cheered. "I want to practice! Help me out here, my new golden friend."

The loom responded by glowing brightly. Lucy began slowly. She placed one elastic after another onto the loom. Using the hook and her fingers she got her rhythm back—over and under, over and under, over and under. This past summer, it had taken Lucy weeks to master the Rainbow Loom art, but today it was a different experience: Lucy felt as if her fingers had wings, so speedily did they fly back and forth. When the ring was finally complete, Lucy felt exhilarated but exhausted. She thought she'd been working for an hour—but when she looked at the clock on her father's desk, only a few minutes had passed. It wasn't even half past two yet!

Lucy placed the ring she'd just made on her finger. It was the most beautiful thing she'd ever seen—it shimmered.

Suddenly, with a *swoosh*, the loom lifted Lucy up and off the window seat. It was like a Ouija board, pulling Lucy where it wanted to go with a mind of its own. With one hand, Lucy held tightly to the loom. With the other, she grabbed for the ebony box. The loom tugged Lucy gently across the old wood floor until she was standing directly in front of her father's bookcase. The loom tapped three times on the fourth shelf where her father kept his collection of rare, antique two hundred-year-old medical texts.

Zap-zap-BANG!

Dust exploded from the old moldy textbooks as if they were angry at being disturbed. Lucy sneezed three times fast. The very next second, the loom began to hum and the bookcase began to wobble. Groaning and weaving back and forth, the bookcase made one last moan before it crashed to the ground.

Lucy was still holding onto the golden loom when she fell unconscious.

Chapter Three

Lucy was awake but she kept her eyes tightly closed. Her head ached a wee bit, as did her forehead, her hands, and her knees, as if her whole body had been used to break a fall. Lucy remembered flying through her father's study and holding on to the magic loom with all the strength she had. She also remembered a humming sound and then, *CRASH! BANG!* The bookcase had fallen and then . . . nothing. Just darkness.

Now she was here—wherever *here* was. Lucy remembered reading in a library book last summer that if you lost your sense of smell, your final end was fast approaching. Lucy took a long deep breath in through her nose to find out if she could expect to live through the afternoon. Yes! She was immediately enveloped with a deep fragrant scent, part tangerine, part jasmine, part alpine meadow. Feeling reassured and safe at last, Lucy opened her eyes slowly, one at a time—and almost began to cry. Not because her knees hurt, or because she wished Alyssa was with her—although both of those things were one hundred percent true—but because she'd been transported to someplace that was not her parents' office.

Lucy was in a field of multicolored peonies—the fragrance was overwhelming. She sat up. The field flowed gently downhill toward a pathway that sparkled as if its pebbles were made of marble and diamonds. The path turned gently and followed a covered bridge over a wide river that flowed with purple water. The path continued on the other side, disappearing into a dark green forest. Far in the distance, hovering over and past the forest trees, was a range of glacier-capped mountains. There the path emerged again, near the top of the second snowcapped mountain peak. Barely visible in the far snowy distance, the path seemed to end at the front door of an emerald green castle. In the late afternoon sunshine, the castle's turrets shimmered gold against a deep turquoise, calm, cloudless sky.

Lucy was dumbfounded. Quickly, she scrunched her eyes closed and counted backward from fifty under her breath. She fully expected to see her own bedroom bookcase when her eyes fluttered open. Instead, she saw only mountains and the peony meadow.

Creak, creak, creak.

Lucy looked behind her. She saw an old fir tree. It had creepy arm-like branches that twisted around each other before reaching toward the mountains and the emerald castle. The tree was massive, and an entryway the size of her parents' office door was carved in its base.

Suddenly Lucy realized the creaking sound was that door beginning to close. She scrambled to her feet and ran to the tree, intending to jam her toe into the doorway to keep the passageway open. She wasn't fast enough. Just as her toe touched the wood, Lucy heard the lock click into place. She tugged desperately on the misshapen green door handle, but it wouldn't budge.

Before she had time to be upset, Lucy was distracted by another sound—the humming song of the magic loom. There, just to the left of the door, it lay hidden in the tree's shadow. The ebony box had tumbled open. The magic loom had fallen out along with a handful of the clear envelopes. The loom was twitching and turning, as if trying to get her attention.

"There you are, my new friend. What in the world has happened to us? Where are we?" Lucy gently picked up the magic loom and rocked it in her arms as if it was a kitten. "You poor thing. Did you think I'd forgotten about you? I would never do that."

In truth, Lucy *had* forgotten about the magic loom for a moment—everything was just so inside out and upside down. This afternoon was crazy! Oh, well. There was no need to upset the odd little thing. Obviously, they were going to have to work together. If Alyssa wasn't around, Lucy and the magic loom needed to get to know each other fast.

"My favorite color is purple," Lucy told her new friend. The magic loom glowed in her arms.

❀ ❀ ❀

After sitting in the sunshine for a time, breathing in the scent of peonies, and wondering how they were going to get home, Lucy decided to take action.

"We can sit here all afternoon waiting until it gets dark, or we can follow the path to the castle and see if someone lives there. Maybe they will help us! Are you with me, friend?" Lucy almost expected the magic loom to reply. Instead, it twitched happily in her hand. "I think that means you agree." With that, Lucy stood, brushed off her pink sweater, and tucked the loom in its ebony box and under her arm. She took one of her deep steadying breaths and marched off through the peonies toward the marble path.

"We've got nothing to lose except our way!" Lucy shouted into the empty, beautiful distance. It wasn't a particularly funny thing to say but Lucy laughed anyway, stoking her courage. She knew at once her giddy shout was a mistake. She watched astounded as her shout transformed into something animated and alive and pinged back and forth across the valley. Like a possessed yodel, it seemed to grow louder and louder instead of fading away. It flew across the valley, shaking the snow out off the treetops on the mountains and scaring a herd of remarkable rainbow-hued zebra-like creatures out of the woods and into a meadow. The shout zigged down the valley, followed the path of the purple river, and headed straight for the covered bridge. Lucy watched, speechless and horrified, as her shout smashed into the side of the bridge and came to a loud, sudden halt.

The world was silent for one moment. Then the floor of the bridge trembled. It heaved. It shuddered. It teetered with one final shaking spasm and fell into the churning, suddenly angry purple water below, doing a spectacular under-over triple axel summersault on the way down.

"Wow," said Lucy, amazed. "Alyssa was right, it never pays to shout."

Lucy couldn't stop staring at the scene in front of her. The bridge was gone. How were they going to get across the river now?

Under her arm, the magic loom glowed. Lucy tapped the box absentmindedly while she focused on coming up with a new plan. She counted backward from twenty-five. Nothing. Lucy's heart began to pound loudly in her chest—never a good sign! Then she noticed the loom humming inside the box, right before it snapped open and fell from under her arm to the ground.

Lucy peered closely at it, wishing her magic loom *could* talk, and that's when she understood. The loom had worked its way out of the box, nudging along a handful of the clear envelopes—the top end of the gold loom lay just across one of them. Its label read *Bridges, Moats, and Turrets*.

"How handy," Lucy said, leaning down to pick it all up. The magic loom hummed happily in response. The elastics in the envelope felt strangely sturdy to the touch—not like a typical elastic—and they were a reassuring dark brown. Lucy didn't like the thought of a bridge being a silly-looking yellow or orange. She laughed out loud, "I'm supposed to weave us a bridge, am I?"

Without waiting for an answer Lucy closed her eyes and imagined the bridge she wanted to create. It was simple-looking, actually. It wasn't a covered bridge, like the one that had floated away. Instead, it was a small suspension bridge, similar to one Lucy crossed last year on a St. Chester's school trip to Bristol. It was called the Clifton Suspension Bridge, and it was over the Avon Gorge. Lucy and Alyssa crossed it together without looking down. Lucy remembered the bridge was narrow and compact, with waist-high handrails made of metal but which looked woven, almost like giant braids of hair. Lucy's eyes popped open. Those cables didn't look much different than a Rainbow Loom bracelet—they were just bigger!

Just as she had done earlier in the afternoon when she wove the ring she was still wearing, Lucy closed her eyes and concentrated. She pictured the suspension bridge in her mind's eye. Lucy reached into the envelope, keeping her eyes shut. As soon as she touched them, the elastics released a strong woodsy scent into the air. As Lucy placed the elastics on the gold loom, the magic loom hummed louder. Her fingers danced over the loom using the hook with new confidence, over and under, under and over, back and forth. They crisscrossed the loom with a will of their own, at lightning speed. The loom was hot now, but Lucy held on. Lucy knew by instinct that if she opened her eyes the spell would be broken—she must be in a trance!

And then, *poof*, it was over. The magic loom dropped from Lucy's fingers and she fell back onto the grass. How much time had passed? She was tired. She counted backward very slowly from ten before she sat up and glanced around.

The sun was in the same place in the sky. Had time stood still? Perhaps it had. There, right before her eyes, was the suspension bridge she imagined, constructed entirely of Rainbow Loom elastics. On the Internet, Lucy and Alyssa had found pictures and YouTube videos of people making elastic clothes and toys, chairs and tables, but she had never seen anything as intricate and impressive as the suspension bridge that just poured itself out of her imagination, onto the gold loom, and into the strange, mysterious world Lucy found herself in.

The bridge stretched from one side of the river to the other. It looked responsible and solid, like a favorite uncle. The magic loom— Lucy was beginning to think of it as an odd cross between a best friend and a pet—hummed happily beside her, proud of their shared accomplishment.

"How about that?" Lucy whispered with excitement, newly afraid to shout. Immediately she was filled with energy and expectation. "Let's cross at once. I can't wait to get to the castle." Lucy picked up the loom and the ebony box. Off they went together across the river to the other side.

Chapter Four

The path glittered beneath Lucy's feet. Here, on the other side of the river, the true splendor of this strange kingdom revealed itself. Overhead, flocks of marvelous red and blue neon-bright birds chattered away to each other in a lilting birdsong. When they noticed Lucy and her ebony box, they swooped down, one after another, to say hello. At first Lucy wanted to duck and hide, but soon she realized the birds were playing with her. Once Lucy relaxed, she held her free arm firmly in front of her, and the strange tiny creatures would alight on her hand or her shoulder, one or two at a time, stealing a free ride. They twittered and chirped joyfully, completely unaware that Lucy didn't under-stand anything they were saying.

As Lucy grew confident and her gait more determined, other creatures popped their heads out from their secret hiding places, from behind bushes and trees to take a good look at the surprise visitor. Lucy could feel their eyes on her—the glowing black eyes of cashmere-soft bright yellow bunnies; the aqua-blue eyes of large, striped chipmunk-like creatures; the shy gaze of deer with bushy pink tails. The creatures followed along behind Lucy, whispering to each other in a lilting, happy, incomprehensible language. Now and then one of the more courageous deer would nudge a nose into the pocket of her pink sweater, looking for a treat. This made Lucy laugh, the sound of which would startle the poor thing and sending it tripping off down the path in alarm.

The farther down the path they traveled away from the fir tree and the passage home, the larger the creatures became. It was very strange. Lucy saw a ginger-striped kitten the size of school bus napping alongside a gerbil the size of Lucy's old toy box! Lucy wondered for a moment if she was shrinking, but when she glanced behind her, the deer and the yellow bunnies had remained the same size. It was as if they had stumbled into a special realm.

As Lucy wandered along with her new menagerie of animal friends, the magic loom remained silent in its ebony carrying case nestled safely under her arm. Lucy supposed it was saving energy for the next challenge—which turned out to be a very good plan.

❀ ❀ ❀

Lucy and the parade of mystical beasts headed steadily uphill toward the dark forest and the mountains. As they marched along, every few minutes Lucy felt the ground tremor. Once, the movement of the earth was so intense, Lucy stumbled and almost lost her balance. The deep shaking sparked unease in the animal ranks and when Lucy looked over her shoulder, she saw that the deer and the chipmunks were, one by one, turning off the path and seeking shelter.

When it happened for the tenth time, Lucy couldn't stand it anymore. She stopped in her tracks, carefully found her balance, and listened. From off in the distance behind her—but clearly getting closer and closer—came a strange thunder-like noise. Lucy turned to look behind her just as the earth began to shake again.

It wasn't thunder Lucy heard, but the deep, outlandish purr of a newly awakened giant. The huge kitten had left the gerbil behind and was now chasing a massive monarch butterfly, all the while creating earthquake-like tremors every time she pounced. Lucy clambered up beside the path and dove behind a bush for safety just as the kitten landed exactly where she'd just been standing, sending pebbles flying. The remainder of the animal parade scattered in fear.

Lucy held tight to the base of the bush with one hand, and to her magic loom with the other. She looked over the top of the bush and watched as the kitten bounced back and forth across the path, causing trees to bend and birds to fly away in terror. Lucy didn't think the kitten was malevolent; she was simply out of control and didn't understand how big she was or how much damage she could do with one flip of her ginger tail.

Lucy had an idea. She needed to distract the kitten and send it prancing off in another direction. If Lucy could accomplish that minor miracle, they could be on their way safely.

The magic loom gently shook, almost like it was laughing—it seemed to know what Lucy was up to. The project Lucy envisioned wasn't as complex as the bridge, but it was going to be huge. Lucy dug around in the box and found the envelope of elastics she was looking for; its label read *Giant Size*.

Lucy sat down behind the bush and again she closed her eyes. She brought to mind an image of the object she wanted to make—a simple ball of string, yes, but this one would be *the mother* of all balls of string! It was going to be gargantuan, made completely of woven Rainbow Loom elastics, but so big and captivating, it would enchant a giant kitten. The project wouldn't require a difficult weave pattern, just perseverance and determination. The magic loom glowed, and Lucy set to work.

Now that Lucy was more comfortable with the process, the trance took over quickly. Her hands flew back and forth over the loom with the glass hook as she made the longest and biggest friendship bracelet this world (or any other) had ever seen. It fell effortlessly off the end of the gold loom and began rolling itself into a ball. Lucy kept at her work. The birds watched, mystified, as the ball grew—it was as big as the bush, then two bushes, then three! Soon it was as large as ten bushes all rolled into one.

Lucy shook her head back and forth to clear her mind, then stood, eager to put her plan into action. The magic loom hummed.

Lucy admired the giant magic loom ball—it was breathtaking. Quickly she positioned herself behind the ball and began to push. It took sixty long seconds, but the ball began to move.

The giant kitten noticed almost at once. Her tail shot straight up and her front paws began to tremble as she readied herself for the game. Lucy stepped back with her fingers crossed behind her back, hoping everything would work as she intended.

The ball picked up speed as it began to roll downhill and onto the path. The kitten half squealed and half purred with delight. Her whole body trembled and her fur bristled with expectation. The kitten concentrated and crouched. She twitched three times and then, *finally,* she jumped. Lucy fell backward as the earth shook with the giant kitten's weight, but when she looked up again, she was thrilled! Just as she hoped, the giant kitten was running downhill after the mother of all balls of string (or elastic). The kitten followed a bend in the path — and was gone.

Mission accomplished! The magic loom hummed in pride and the animals cheered as they emerged from hiding. Lucy picked herself up and took a deep theatrical bow. Then they were off. There wasn't a moment to waste.

Chapter Five

Lucy felt uneasy as soon as they arrived at the edge of the forest. And when the glittering path turned mossy and damp, Lucy's stomach did a somersault. She hated dark corners, spooky stories, and cobwebs. Spiders and snakes were completely off-limits. Once, Alyssa had shared with Lucy that she wanted to be a zoologist when she grew up—Lucy was horrified. If that meant Alyssa would be working with bats, slithery things, and creepy-crawlers, Lucy wondered out loud if they could stay friends. Alyssa explained she wanted to work with *primates*—gorillas and monkeys and the like—not snakes! Lucy remembered how relieved she had been at hearing the news.

Alyssa had come to mind just now because Lucy was nervous. Lucy always felt fearless when her best friend was with her—she really believed that together they could get through anything! But Alyssa wasn't here. And her new animal friends weren't behaving like heroes at the moment. The bunnies, deer, and chipmunks were all huddled together in a haphazard cluster, whimpering fearfully and loudly. If she entered the dark forest, Lucy suspected she would be traveling alone. Well, not *entirely* alone. The magic loom would come with her, obviously. Together, the two of them were proving to be quite the A-team! For a moment Lucy felt better.

Just then, the herd of rainbow-colored zebra-like animals Lucy spotted earlier in the afternoon came stampeding out of the dark forest, knocking Lucy over and sending the ebony box flying.

"Please be careful," Lucy shouted, newly frazzled. "Watch where you're going." Lucy scrambled along on her hands and knees until she found the ebony box.

"Oh, my. Oh, no. Oh, dear. What have we done?" asked the leader of the herd, a grandmotherly nervous creature whose rainbow-colored coat was tinged with silver and gray. "Did you scrape your knee?"

It had been so long since Lucy had heard a real live voice, her eyes welled up with tears.

"Oh, my. Oh, no. Please do not cry! I won't be able to stand it—and then we'll all start crying and cause a very serious flood. Don't laugh. It's happened before. As a species we're both sensitive and skittish. It's exhausting."

The creature handed Lucy a striped hanky. Lucy blew her nose.

"Hello. My name is Lucy Stillwater-Smith. I am very pleased to meet you," said Lucy, remembering her manners.

The zebra tilted her head to one side and looked Lucy up and down.

"Are you a little girl?" she asked.

"I'm not *that* little," Lucy replied.

"Are you a little girl?" she asked again.

"Who wants to know?" Lucy replied, suddenly suspicious.

"Don't be like that. I've only ever seen one other little girl in my whole life and her fur was a different color than yours. Maybe you are another species altogether. How am I supposed to know?"

"Little girls don't have fur," Lucy replied stiffly.

"What's that on your head? It looks like brown fur to me. The other one has fur that is a lovely shade of red."

"It's not fur. It's hair!"

"May I touch it?"

"No, you may not touch my hair. That's a very rude thing to ask."

"Why is that rude? If we're to be friends, we have to get to know each other. You can ask me anything at all."

"I have a lot of questions. What's the fastest way to the castle? Who lives there? Are they nice? Are you planning to help me or eat me?"

"Well, for starters, I don't eat meat. No worries, there. Zebras are one hundred percent vegetarian all the way!"

Lucy looked around to see all of the other neon-stripped zebras encircling them while they chatted. "Then why did you come running at me?"

"We were sent to help you safely on your way. We seem to have arrived just in time," she said. With obvious agitation she looked nervously at the entrance to the dark forest.

"Who sent you? And why just in time?" Lucy asked excitedly, but worried.

"I can't tell you anything more because she wants to explain everything to you. All you need to know is this: you *must not* step foot in the forest. It's allergic to little girls. The reaction happened just once before—the forest begins wheezing and sneezing. The trees drip and ooze all over the path until it's completely clogged in a nasty yellow goo that clogs everything up and lasts forever. Trust me, my luv, it's a big old mess. You must find another way through the forest."

Just then, the birds decided it was time to join the conversation. *Whoosh.* They fluttered from behind the cloud where they'd been hiding, and swooped down to greet the zebras. The unexpected flurry of activity and the noisy beating of the little bird wings spooked the skittish herd. The zebras froze in blind terror, and then took off together down the path and back toward the bridge.

"Oh, no! Oh, dear! I am getting much too old for this," the zebra muttered. "I mustn't stay a minute longer. I have to run after the others and make sure they're okay. It was lovely to meet you, Lucy Stillwater-Smith. Remember, you cannot walk through the forest safely."

And she was gone.

The birds twittered sheepishly. Lucy sat down in the tall grass at the edge of the forest, confused and exhausted. What was she supposed to do now? This was truly the longest and most confusing afternoon of her life so far. Lucy was considering the pros of having a comforting cry when the magic loom began to glow under her arm. That's when it came to her.

Lucy placed the ebony box in the grass and opened it up. She took out the magic loom and placed it gently in her lap. She flipped through the collection of envelopes looking for the one she remembered seeing earlier in the day. There it was!

Once again, Lucy crossed her legs and closed her eyes. In her mind's eye, Lucy drew an intricate and detailed picture of the prettiest little red and blue bird. Soon she had a crystal clear image of what she would create with her magic loom—a pair of glittering wings with a matching harness system. Voilà! How hard could that be?

Lucy opened the envelope and organized everything she needed, the blue and red elastics and the glass hook. This newest envelope was labeled *Flights of Fancy*. She was ready.

For the fourth time this afternoon, Lucy fell into a deep trance. Her nimble, strong fingers wove with clear determination, precision, and speed. The animals watched in awe as wings slowly revealed themselves and fell fully formed to the ground. And then, just like before, Lucy was suddenly awake and exhausted. She was afraid to look.

Lucy counted backward from ten and opened her eyes wide. She saw a set of exquisite wings. They had a twenty-five-foot span and were made entirely of blue and red elastics with intricate, billowing elastic feathers. The wings were attached to a series of broad Rainbow Loom ties—ties for her wrists, her elbows, her shoulders, and her waist. Lucy's heart pounded. Was it possible the plan could work?

"I don't think I can do this all by myself," Lucy said, raising her gaze to the birds circling above her. "You gave me the idea—are you willing to help with the execution?"

Their response was instantaneous. The birds flew down to the ties, grabbing the ends in their beaks. They circled around Lucy. One after another, in perfect sync, they zipped back and forth, attaching the Rainbow Loom wings to Lucy's back, hands, and arms, crisscrossing the ties and then pulling them snug.

"Can they be any tighter?" Lucy asked nervously. "Will you show me how to do this? I want to fly over the forest without triggering the allergic reaction. I want to get home tonight—not in two hundred years. Can you help me, friends?"

One of the birds held on to the magic loom with her beak and dropped it into the ebony box. She twittered for a friend to join, and the two birds skipped together down the path before lifting off into the air, the magic loom cradled between them.

"That doesn't look hard," Lucy said with more confidence than she felt. She took a deep breath and mimicked what the birds had just done, running with all of her power toward the forest. At the edge of the darkness, just as Lucy thought she might crash into the trees, the wind found her Rainbow Loom wings. Lucy was lifted into the sky, surrounded on all sides by the birds chirping encouragement.

Flying was the most wonderful feeling. Lucy had been expecting it to be scary, but it wasn't frightening at all. It was more like floating in water than riding a roller coaster. Lucy didn't have to flap her new wings very hard. She simply tilted them at an angle to the wind and was carried up and over the forest. No wonder birds made a racket at dawn—who wouldn't want to be up and about if flying was this much fun?

Lucy wanted to glide all the way to the castle, but unfortunately she made a big mistake—she looked at the ground. Just thinking about gravity deactivated the magic. Slowly, Lucy began to lose altitude. She drifted past the edge of the forest and was soon sitting safely in a meadow of sunflowers. Lucy watched sadly as her beautiful magic loom wings and ties melted away in the sun. Well, that sure was a blast! And she hadn't caused an allergic reaction in the forest.

The birds fluttered above Lucy's head. They dropped the boxed magic loom softly in Lucy's lap and flew off happily toward the mountain. The castle was closer than it had been all afternoon!

Chapter Six

Lucy stared at the wall of mountains in front of her. They were daunting peaks, wild and ragged-looking. They wouldn't suffer fools gladly, as Abigail would say.

For the first time all afternoon, Lucy's stomach growled. She wondered suddenly what was happening at 163 Terrier Square. Lucy missed everyone—her mum, her dad, and Abigail. The feeling was big, messy, and lonely. Because the Stillwater-Smiths were a self-reliant, independent bunch, Lucy wondered if anybody even noticed she was gone. Often on Saturday night the Doctors organized a date night. Leaving Lucy and Abigail at home eating fish and chips takeout, they went to a nice restaurant for curry. If Lucy's parents went to dinner straight from the hospital this evening, would they even miss her? And what if they forgot to pop their heads in to say goodnight just because they were tired or, worse, they were still mad? And Lucy had almost forgot: it was the first Saturday in November, the day Abigail made her monthly trek to visit her sister Bebe! What if Abigail left Lucy's tea outside her bedroom door, then made a mad dash to catch the two forty-five train at Russell Square station? Homesickness and worry wormed their way into Lucy's heart. What if no one missed her? What if couldn't find her way home? What if she never saw Alyssa again?

Lucy squeezed her eyes tight together. She counted backward from one hundred. There simply wasn't enough time to get upset worrying about a bunch of what-ifs. Dr. Smith often said that a good attitude and an optimistic, happy heart solved more problems than a grain of worry ever did. When things got scary or hard, it was important not to let oneself get rattled. The practical solution to a tough challenge was always to march through it with the help of a solid plan and a big dose of hard work. Lucy could hear her mother and father chanting the Stillwater-Smith family mantra: *Solving difficult problems is fun — let's just get on with it and make the world a better place!*

Lucy jumped to her feet. If she was going make it home sooner rather than later, she'd better get a move on. "Onward and upward, Miss Lucy Stillwater-Smith," she hummed to herself. "You are on an adventure . . . and everything is going to work out. I know it deep in my bones, just like I knew the package was meant for me."

❀ ❀ ❀

The path on this side of the forest continued to glitter, but it was steep now and getting steeper. Lucy decided to view the incline as positive even if she was huffing and puffing. If she was heading up, that meant the castle was getting closer every minute. She knew she was heading in the right direction because there hadn't been a fork in the road along the way, not once.

Lucy wondered who lived in the castle. Taking her mother's example as her inspiration, Lucy chose to feel excited about the afternoon in front of her, not uneasy. As if in encouragement, the magic loom glowed under her arm. It couldn't be far now. Lucy turned a bend in the path and her heart did an excited triple somersault. There it was!

Up close, the castle was breathtaking! It was perched on the side of a steep cliff. The castle had six turrets and was surrounded on all sides by a moat filled with water. Earlier, when Lucy first saw the castle, she thought it was green. Now she saw that its walls were actually made of dark stone and covered with thick green vines that appeared centuries old. Lucy saw small yellow climbing flowers blooming here and there on the old walls, mixed in with the vines. The flowers gave off a heady, happy scent similar to the old-fashioned English tea roses Abigail loved so much—spicy and sweet all at the same time. Each wall had six wide windows positioned high above the water. A pretty flower box sat at the base of each window, overflowing with trailing white blooms and sprays of pink foliage. The castle's front door was twenty feet high, arched at the top, and had green and blue stained glass windowpanes that twinkled in the low light.

There was a small ledge made of dark gray stone beneath the door with just enough room for one person to stand and knock. Even so, Lucy wondered if she could reach the knocker. The overall effect was magical. The castle looked as if it could be the home of someone friendly and not an evil dragon or an icy witch. Admiring the view, Lucy felt immensely better. But there was one teeny tiny little problem. There wasn't a bridge over the moat!

Lucy worried as she opened the ebony box. If she had known about the moat, she wouldn't have used her one and only magic bridge! She flipped through the envelopes, looking for the right label, something that could help. She found a catapult and a ladder—both reasonable possibilities she supposed. She also found instructions for making a winged horse and an invisibility cloak that she'd missed before or forgotten about. Lucy knew she was beginning to get tired because both ideas sounded too complicated. She found envelopes promising lassoes, tents, a bicycle and even a tree house. Every envelope sparkled with endless possibilities, but Lucy was so intent on finding another bridge she couldn't see the magic right in front of her.

Suddenly Lucy knew what she wanted to do. She would weave a trampoline! In a jiffy,

Lucy's good mood returned and so did her energy. Lucy and Alyssa were trampoline champions. Not only was this the solution to the problem at hand, but it had the potential to be awesome fun. She pulled out the elastics labeled *Bounce*.

Lucy closed her eyes. She imagined the back garden at 163 Terrier Square. She saw the stone wall at the end of the garden, covered in pink climbing roses. She conjured up the image of Abigail sitting on the raised stone terrace behind her, watching and drinking the green tea from India that Dr. Stillwater had brought home from one of his trips. Lucy could see the trampoline in front of her, clear as day, with its wide bouncing platform and the black wood ladder her father built so Lucy and Alyssa could climb up more easily. Lucy imagined she was standing in the center of the trampoline holding Alyssa's two hands in her own. The feeling was so real, she almost opened her eyes to peek, but stopped herself in time. The gold loom hummed with delight.

This trampoline was going to have a bounce the girls had only ever dreamed of. With no trouble at all, they would have been able to bounce high above the house on Terrier Square and up into the clouds. Lucy could see it all so clearly. Together the girls would perform ten back-flips each, bounce twice more as they slowed down, and finally, for the big finish, cartwheel into handstands at the trampoline's edge before making a perfectly synchronized dismount. Lucy imagined she could hear Abigail applauding in the background and shouting "Ten! Ten! Ten!" as if the girls were Olympic athletes with a world-record-breaking perfect score.

The magic loom hummed louder and Lucy was brought out of her dreaming. She fell back into the trance as her fingers reached for the loom.

And then it was over. This time Lucy was afraid to open her eyes. What she wanted to see was her Terrier Square backyard and the dusty old trampoline of her childhood with its lovingly homemade ladder. She didn't want to stay trapped in this mysterious world of invention and transformation forever. Was she ever going to get home?

Lucy couldn't afford to feel tired, defeated, and distracted by homesickness. Her eyes remained closed, and the magic loom serenaded her with a soft, confident hum of support in an effort to replenish Lucy's resources. The hum trickled into Lucy's heart and cheered her. She wasn't really all alone after all—she was only momentarily tired and overwhelmed. Lucy knew she would get through with the help of her new friends and the magic loom. Confidence restored, Lucy slowly opened her eyes.

The trampoline was a masterpiece. Lucy stepped tentatively onto the multicolor steps she had created and walked forward. The trampoline's weave was tight and even. Lucy tested its elasticity with her foot and the give was remarkable—strong but generous. It was twice the size of the trampoline in Lucy's backyard at home and was positioned at the edge of the moat, exactly where it needed to be for Lucy's plan to work.

"All I have to do is bounce gently," Lucy said to herself in a confident coach voice she didn't know she possessed until just this moment. "And my landing can't be too hard. I need to bounce high enough to land exactly at the top of the castle wall. Just imagine yourself doing it. Swing your arms hard and bend your knees deeply. You've got this."

The water in the moat was deep and dangerous-looking. Lucy looked up at the castle wall instead of down. She counted backward from twenty-five and began. She bounced gently as planned, building up height and power ever so slowly. It took three big bounces to reach as high as the castle door, and then five more to reach past the row of window boxes. Lucy's bird friends perched at the edge of the castle wall, chirping and cheering her on. She bounced higher and higher still, until she was hovering near the top of the wall before gravity pulled her down again. The next bounce would be the winner.

As she touched down on the trampoline, Lucy sank into its strength, then shot straight up and into the sky. With her legs loose and her arms tucked at her sides, she floated above the wall, exactly where she needed to be. Lucy tucked into a somersault, reaching down to cushion herself, and then landed suddenly, with a rough jolt, on the passageway near the top of the wall. The landing wasn't the gentle perfect ten she hoped for, but she made it!

Lucy stood and looked around. She was so pleased with herself, it took a minute or two before she noticed: far below in the castle's center courtyard a figure was kneeling—and pointing a bow directly at her head. That was also the moment Lucy realized the magic loom was resting beside the trampoline far below, completely forgotten.

Chapter Seven

Lucy ducked just as an arrow flew over the edge of the wall. These castle folk clearly weren't as friendly as she had hoped.

Lucy was nestled against a cold wall on one side of a narrow passageway open to the sky. It was intended, Lucy supposed, as fortification. To her right and left, steps led to small stone platforms where one could imagine watchmen standing guard—luckily they were abandoned at present. Lucy suddenly realized that castle walls and windows she had seen from far below weren't the real castle. Rather, their intended purpose was to hide and protect a large, wide courtyard and the jewel-box castle nestled within.

Whoosh.

Another arrow flew over Lucy's head. This was ridiculous! If she hadn't been so upset, Lucy would have laughed. She hadn't come all this way to be pierced in the head by an arrow. All she wanted was to find a way home. And now—just because she was distracted for one measly minute—she didn't have her magic loom! If she had it in hand where it was supposed to be, she would whip up a magic loom lasso, hog-tie the archer below, and talk some sense into the person who was shooting arrows at her. Oh, dear.

Just then Lucy's bird chums began chirping intently. In her agitation Lucy had forgotten about them, but they hadn't forgotten about her. Her two favorites were trying to catch Lucy's eye without attracting the figure in the courtyard.

Initially Lucy couldn't understand what the birds were trying to tell her. They flapped their wings and levitated just above the stone path. They were pecking at each other in an odd little pantomime, trying to hold Lucy's attention. And then she understood!

"Yes, yes, yes! That's a brilliant idea. You two should fly down to the other side of the moat. If you're able to carry and return the ebony box to me without being noticed, you'll save the day. I know you can do it."

The birds didn't waste any time. They dashed over the wall and glided down to the moat's edge where the magic loom was alone beside the trampoline. Lucy crawled on her stomach to the other side of the passageway where there was a small slit in the stone just big enough for her to peer through.

Lucy held her breath as she watched their maneuvers. At first the two birds attempted to share the weight of the box between them. They tried to position themselves at opposite ends of the box while nestling themselves underneath it in the hope they could flap their wings and rise. Unfortunately, the loom was behaving erratically after being left alone by the side of the moat, and kept twisting and turning. Each time it did, one of the birds would startle and drop their end, and they would be forced to start all over again. This happened three times before the smallest bird called in additional support.

Down swooped six of their friends. The others flew around close to the ground, zipping back and forth over the grass, hunting for something. Lucy wondered what they were looking for until she saw two birds return to the edge of the moat with large, sturdy twigs in their beaks, much like they would use to build a nest. Working as a team, the little flock of birds nudged twigs under the ebony box until it was perfectly balanced. Then they divided into teams of four and positioned themselves on either side of the box, each one holding on to a twig. They chirped loudly in unison as if in a countdown and slowly began to flutter their wings and rise. Lucy held her breath as they lifted off the ground, quickly and sound-lessly. They rose past the doorway and then the windows, before dropping their precious cargo gently at Lucy's feet, all without being noticed by the archer below. Before she opened the box to make sure the magic loom was OK, Lucy blew each one of the birds a kiss. Happily, the magic loom was safe: it glowed thankfully, eager to get to work.

Lucy pondered her options. She could create a lasso and tie the archer up, pretending she was an American cowgirl subduing a bull. Or she could make a ladder and shimmy down to the courtyard. Would she be too easy to see if she chose that option? Maybe an invisible cloak could keep her safe long enough to climb down the ladder. That might work. But Lucy wondered if she should save the invisibility trick for an emergency—she had a long way to go before she got home. Maybe the first idea was the best after all? While Lucy focused on coming up with the perfect plan, arrows flew over her head. She had to do something fast.

Lucy edged herself into a corner. Snuggled between the passageway wall and one of the platforms, she was protected by a slight over-hang. She reached into the box and shuffled through the remaining envelopes looking for the *Magic Lasso* label. There it was! The lasso elastics were sturdy and deep royal blue. Lucy closed her eyes and imagined the magnificent object she wanted to create—it would be elab-orate, large, and able to execute a breathtak-ing series of cowboy rustler tricks, the likes of which had never been seen before this side of Kansas City. The magic loom hissed with delight. Lucy smiled and fell into one of her trances. Her fingers flew back and forth while the hook weaved its Western miracle. A flash of rainbow colored sparks signaled it was over and Lucy's eyes opened.

For the plan to work, Lucy knew she had to be precise about the next step. Lucy popped her head over the wall, quickly trying to get a better sense of where the archer was positioned. She moved onto her feet but stayed bent at the knees, keeping her head low. Next, she carefully gathered the lasso between her elbow and arm in a series of overlapping circles. She and Alyssa had watched cowboys do this in a rodeo documentary about the Calgary Stampede. Lucy didn't have time to practice and she was worried about her aim, but the magic loom hadn't failed her yet. She would toss the lasso with gusto and choose to have faith.

Lucy was almost ready. She patted the magic loom with her spare hand for good luck and counted backward from ten. Hoping she could throw the archer off guard, she yelled loudly and jumped up. Then, she threw the lasso with all the strength she could muster and let go.

Lucy bopped her head up and watched as the lasso nosedived directly into the castle courtyard with unwavering zeal. It headed straight for the archer, who appeared to stumble backward. The archer dropped the bow, and the lasso wrapped itself around the archer's hands and feet.

Lucy cheered, grabbed the ebony case, and headed straight for a stairway. Home was getting closer every minute, she could feel it!

Chapter Eight

Lucy bounded down the stairs, almost running. The staircase curved around one corner and then another. The air was old and musty, as if the stairwell had been blocked off for eons and just recently opened up. When Lucy finally reached the bottom of the stairs, she found herself in a wide open doorway, staring out into the old castle courtyard.

The courtyard was beautiful. Intricate stone paths led the way through a series of wide gardens that edged the thick castle walls. The spicy scent of the yellow flowers was still here, but now it was mixed with the fragrance of rosemary, oregano, thyme, and lavender. The area was the size of four, maybe five, soccer fields. Lucy could now see clearly that the center of the courtyard—where the archer had been kneeling—was actually a maze made of huge holly hedges. Behind the maze Lucy could just make out the outline of the smaller castle.

Lucy headed straight for the maze, confident she would find the lassoed troublemaker at its center. Before entering, Lucy opened the ebony box. She dug around, hunting for an envelope containing simple, straightforward elastics. She planned to drop them in a trail behind her, to make sure she could find her way back.

Lucy stepped into the maze and stopped. She listened. Above her, the flock of red and blue birds twittered, offering, it seemed to Lucy, to guide their friend to the center of the maze. Lucy could hear a faint whimpering, almost like the sound of a kitten crying. She headed in.

Inside the maze, it was dark. The sweet scent of lavender was quickly overtaken by a dank mossy smell. The hedges seemed taller on the inside of the maze than they had from the outside. Lucy was overtaken with a feeling of claustrophobia, as if the hedge walls could collapse in on her at any moment. It took everything she had to keep moving forward. What she really wanted to do was turn on her heel and run back toward the warm afternoon sunlight. To keep her wits about her, Lucy gazed at the sky and the birds. When she came to a fork in the path, she asked the birds for guidance and they led her fearlessly forward. With every turn, the whimpering sound grew louder.

And then, suddenly, Lucy was in a wide clearing. Directly in front of her, wrapped in a bundle on the ground, was the archer she had seen from the wall. The person who had seemed menacing and mean from a great distance was now helpless, tangled up, and crying like a little kitten. Lucy almost laughed out loud, but stopped herself just in time. She didn't want to be nasty after all, she just wanted to get home!

"Are you all right?" Lucy asked rather stiffly. "I'm sorry about the fuss and bother, but you started it."

The archer didn't move or make a sound.

"It wasn't nice of you to point your bow at my head. *Shooting* arrows at me was downright rude. You didn't even attempt to be welcoming."

Lucy waited for the archer to indicate polite regret with a heartfelt groan or an embarrassed twitch, but nothing happened.

"Oh, dear. Don't be like that. The truth is I need help *desperately*. I promise I'm not an enemy, even if all this commotion feels rather aggressive. I am deeply sorry if that happens to be the case, but I wasn't sure what else to do. My name is Lucy Stillwater-Smith. I promise I don't want to take anything that is yours. I simply want help finding my way back to 163 Terrier Square, London."

The word "London" was the ticket, or maybe it was "Terrier Square"—anyway, all at once the archer began to rock back and forth as if it was attempting to kick loose what Lucy now realized was a dirty old emerald cape. The magic lasso had managed to tie the cape firmly in place, keeping the archer's face completely hidden from Lucy's view.

"If I untie you, will you consider being helpful? Or are you committed to ending my life?"

The figure seemed to nod.

"Well, which one is it?" Lucy asked. "Nasty or nice? Nod twice if nice is the plan."

The hooded figure presented Lucy with two concise but vigorous nods of the head.

"Well, that's that then. Let's have bygones be bygones—as Abigail would say if she were with us—and get this lasso off you."

Lucy was about to kneel down on all fours and carefully untie the lasso with her hands when the magic loom began to hum happily and loudly. Lucy suspected the untying process wasn't going to be very hard. She reached down with one hand and gave the end of lasso a firm tug. That's all it took. The woven rope disintegrated with a quick *poof* and a blast of cold air. The sudden gust was all it took to knock the emerald hood off the head of the figure on the ground.

Lucy wasn't sure what she was expecting to see, but it definitely wasn't what appeared in front of her. Instead of an angry watchman, Lucy saw a small redheaded girl with two pretty braids. The girl looked terrified.

"Please, please don't be angry!" she cried. "I am sorry if I frightened you, but you frightened me first!"

Lucy grimaced at her.

"No, really, it's true," the girl said defensively. "No one has visited me here before, except the zebras, and then only once. I thought if I didn't allow the bridge to drop over the moat,

79

I would have time to figure out what to do and how to behave. But when you leaped to the castle wall, I was flabbergasted. I was scared." The girl paused. "Perhaps I may have overreacted."

"Aiming arrows at my skull does seem like an overreaction," Lucy snapped. "Now that I can see you better, you should also know that the cloak and dagger costume is a bit much. Up this close, you look silly."

"Don't you think it's a terrifying shade of emerald?" the girl asked with sudden curiosity and seriousness. "The wizard who lived here before me—a nasty fellow, I'm told—left it behind. I put it on whenever I need an extra bit of confidence." And then she laughed. "I am truly sorry. I think I spend too much time by myself. My name is Sallee Ratchford-Jones the Third. How do you do?"

With that the girl stood up, pulled the cloak to the ground and made quick little curtsey in Lucy's general direction. Beneath the cloak, Sallee was dressed in an old-fashioned dark brown muslin dress with two pretty rows of pearl buttons that traveled up the front of the bodice to the tip of her smudged chin. She wore a pair of black lace-up boots. Bright green silk bows were tied neatly at the tips of her two long braids. Her hair was a vibrant, happy shade of red. Lucy loved the color immediately. In comparison, Lucy's comfy pink sweater with pockets, her purple skirt, and black flats looked like a costume from another century.

Lucy curtsied as best she could, feeling slightly silly. "I am pleased to meet you, Sallee."

The girls stared at each other awkwardly for a few moments, unsure of where to go next with the conversation. Lucy didn't feel like she had time to waste, whereas Sallee wasn't convinced she wanted to be friends with the strange-looking creature standing in front of her.

"What happened to your dress?" Sallee asked, in what she hoped was a polite voice.

"Excuse me?" Lucy replied. It wasn't clear to her what the girl was talking about.

"Why is your skirt so short? And what is on your legs?"

"I'm wearing extremely comfortable pants underneath. You could also call them leggings. I don't like blue jeans. Why does it matter?" Lucy wanted to get on with things and was running out of patience with the direction the conversation was taking.

"Girls don't wear pants."

"Excuse me?"

"Girls don't wear pants," Sallee repeated loudly, as if she was talking to someone wearing earplugs.

"What are you talking about? Of course girls wear pants," Lucy almost shouted.

The girls said nothing more—they simply stared. They were standing an arm's length away from each other in the center of the maze. The birds were fluttering happily above their heads. The magic loom in its ebony case was tucked firmly under Lucy's arm, glowing more and more with every passing second. Lucy was wearing her favorite Saturday outfit with her long brown hair pulled off her face in a ponytail. Sallee, the new girl, appeared to be dressed in an old-fashioned doll costume. *Sallee.* Where had Lucy heard that name before?

What in the world was going on?

Chapter Nine

"Are you expecting a package?" Lucy asked.

Sallee tilted her head, looked Lucy up and down, appeared flustered, and then began to cry. In no time at all, she was wailing. And Sallee wasn't a delicate, pretty weeper like Alyssa. Instead, her lovely face became instantly red and blotchy before puffing up like a soggy marshmallow. She made loud gasping noises between wails, as if she couldn't catch her breath, and then sat down in a puddle of frustration and sadness.

"Oh, dear. Are you OK?" Lucy looked around to find something Sallee could blow her nose on. She spotted the wizard's emerald cloak in a lump on the ground and tugged it over to where Sallee was sitting. "Blow on this," she suggested. "I am sure he wouldn't mind."

Lucy sat down beside Sallee in the dirt and placed her arm around the other girl's shoulder. This made Sallee wail louder still. Then, with one final damp snort, the girl's tears ran out.

"I can't stand it here anymore," Sallee said, wiping her eyes on the sleeve of her brown muslin dress. "I'm lonely and time passes so slowly here, if it passes at all. I can't tell you if it's the nature of things in this place, or if it's because I have been so alone for so long."

"I'm starting to think I've been sent here to help you, Sallee. You didn't answer my question just now. Are you waiting for a package?"

All this time the magic loom in its ebony and mother-of-pearl box had been quiet. Now that Sallee had calmed down, it seemed to think it was time to join the conversation. Ever so softly, a sweet gentle hum began. The box glowed, and color leaked from its corners, floating above the girls' heads before transforming into multicolored bubbles—almost like bath bubbles—above their heads.

"Good gracious," Sallee said, startled. "What on earth is that?"

Lucy laughed. "It's the magic loom trying to get our attention. I thought it was mine, but now I think it may have been looking for you all this time! Tell me your story. Have you always lived here?"

"Oh my, no! I've been trapped here by mistake. I live in London, on Terrier Square, with my mum and dad. They're inventors."

"But so do I! I live at 163 Terrier Square. Which house is yours?"

"That's *my* house, silly! And I want to get back there right this minute!"

The magic loom was having fit inside the ebony box. Finally it pushed at the lid with a huge shove and tumbled out at Lucy's feet.

Lucy barely noticed. She was thinking so hard she wondered if smoke was coming out of her ears.

"What year is it, Sallee?"

"I beg your pardon?"

"What year is it? Today! Who is the queen?"

"What a ridiculous question. Queen Victoria, of course. She's been Queen since before I was born."

"What year is it, Sallee? Tell me right now!"

"It is 1884. And yes, it's Saturday and it's November. What is this all about? Have you figured it all out?"

"Sallee," Lucy said very quietly, "please tell me everything—and quickly if you can. What exactly happened to you today?"

"As you wish. Here's the whole sad story in a nutshell: My friend Liza moved to America last week. Her ship sailed on Tuesday and I have been horribly lonely ever since. This morning it was raining very hard. I went for my walk in the park anyway, even though a gale was blowing. The tea shop was closed, but I saw old Mrs. Gloucester waving at me from her bay window overlooking the park. I love her *and* her dog— the two of them always manage to make me feel better. Why not pop in for a quick cup of tea?"

Lucy interrupted: "Is her dog Mr. Poppins, a gray Bouvier? Are Mrs. Gloucester's spectacles brown tortoiseshell?"

"Yes on both counts." She could tell Lucy was getting excited so she continued. The words tumbled out of her at breakneck speed. "Mrs. Gloucester is sweet and cheery but so absentminded. While we were drinking tea and eating sweets, she asked if I could return a library book to my father's shelves without him noticing. She said she had borrowed the book from my father last year and simply forgotten to return it. Now she was too embarrassed to do it herself. I was happy to do it, of course. The book was a huge tattered antique thing and she told me it lived on the fourth shelf of the second bookcase. She wrapped it in a striped cotton sheet before I left so it wouldn't get wet on the walk home. Abbey, our housemaid, opened the door at 163 when I knocked—with the old book in my arms I couldn't reach the bell—and I ran up the stairs to my father's library. He and my mum spend most days working at the British Museum around the corner, so I didn't knock—I just charged in. I unwrapped the book, found the fourth shelf, stood on my tippy-toes and slid the book into one of the open spaces on the shelf. Suddenly the bookcase began to tilt and dust exploded everywhere. I began to sneeze, fell over backward—and that's the last thing I remember. The next thing I knew I was in a field of flowers, surrounded on all sides by a herd of colorful zebras. One of them woke me up by licking my arm. It was sort of gross."

Lucy wanted to ask a question, but Sallee shushed her with a quick wave of her hand. "There's so much more to this story so let me finish. This is what the zebra told me: I'd managed to place the book in the wrong opening on the bookshelf. When the spines of these two old alchemy books touched, an unprecedented chemical reaction was created—Mrs. Gloucester was sure of it. It turns out Mrs. Gloucester is a complicated and very old soul. She and Mr. Poppins are from this world, and not from London. She flitters between this place and Terrier Square through a secret door in her attic. She thought hers was the only entrance that existed until the explosion in our library revealed another one. When I messed up the order of the old books and the entryway in our library appeared, the passage in her house snapped shut. For a few hours she could chat through her closed door to the terrified old zebra, but after I set off an allergic reaction by stepping in the forest by mistake, even that line of communication clogged up. The zebra explained everything she could before pointing me to this castle. The bridge was down over the moat when I arrived and I just wandered in. I have been here all day wondering what to do next. And then you arrived."

Lucy's eyes were as wide as two harvest moons. Mrs. Gloucester had always been very nice to Lucy, but she was having trouble accepting the sweet little old lady she knew was a time-traveling adventurer from another world. That said, it almost made a tiny bit of sense. Mrs. Gloucester hadn't been in the park this morning, and she was *always* in the park that time of the day. Mrs. Gloucester also knew Lucy well enough to know she would be enchanted by a mysterious package. Perhaps only girls could travel through the new passageway whereas old ladies could travel through the old one? That made some sense. That also meant Mrs. Gloucester needed Lucy's help to sort out the mess. Sending Lucy the magic loom had been a good idea. Mrs. Gloucester knew how much Lucy loved weaving, because Lucy made Mr. Poppins a stunning and intricate Rainbow Loom leash last summer. But how had Lucy and Sallee slid through the portal on the very same day—but in two different centuries? This was all very mysterious!

Sallee and Lucy shared just one more problem in common: what were they going to do now?

Chapter Ten

Lucy and Sallee were still sitting side by side in the center of maze. The magic loom was out of its box and humming expectantly by Lucy's side, waiting for the next set of instructions. Both girls looked the worse for wear. In the excitement of telling her story, Sallee had lost one of her bows and she still had dirt on her nose. Lucy had scraped holes in the knees of her leggings crawling around on the floor of the castle wall. Both girls should have been exhausted, but instead they were re-energized and excited to tackle the problem. Two was definitely better than one.

They had a zillion questions to ask each other. Sallee wanted to know what had changed at Terrier Square over the last hundred years.

She suspected Lucy could tell her what the future held in store—would she invent something that cured sick children? Would she live in London her whole life? Would she enter Oxford and study math? Was she going to have children? Who would be her first love? Could Lucy tell her all these things and more? And then, as suddenly as Sallee realized Lucy might know the answers to all of these questions, she realized she didn't want to know the answers to her questions. Not knowing what wonderful thing might happen next was one of the things Sallee loved most. Just this afternoon she'd been about to give up, when all of a sudden, Lucy was there to save the day. There was no way she wanted to live her whole life without ever being surprised again. She decided not to ask.

Lucy on the other had was filled with grand plans: Sallee was going to be a great resource for Lucy's next history test. Lucy enjoyed hearing people tell their stories about the past out loud much more than reading history—she remembered everything so much better. She could learn so much from Sallee.

More than anything else right now though, the girls needed to get home . . . and to the right century. And Lucy had a plan.

"Here's what we're going to do. In the ebony box is an envelope labeled *Catapult*. I noticed it earlier this morning. And that is what I am going to make right now." She grabbed Sallee's arm with one hand and picked up the magic loom with the other.

"Where are we going?" Sallee asked, confused by sudden flurry of movement.

"We're following the elastics I dropped out of the maze and heading into the larger courtyard. We need more room. Then I am going to get to work."

❁ ❁ ❁

Lucy had only ever seen a catapult once before, one day last summer when the Stillwater-Smiths took Lucy, Alyssa, and Abigail to a medieval fair in the countryside near Oxfordshire. They saw a play, watched maypole dancers, and ate the most delicious raspberry pudding. Near the end of the afternoon, there was a competition between local towns. Two amateur carpentry clubs had built catapults from a set of antique plans a librarian had discovered in the stacks.

That afternoon the clubs had competed to see which town's catapult could toss a large rock the farthest. Lucy's plan was to switch things up in an interesting way—she was going to create a catapult sturdy enough to toss Lucy and Sallee all the way over the sunflower meadow, through the forest, past the peonies to the fir tree and the doorway to home. "How hard could that be?" Lucy whispered to herself, gulping down her doubts. Any plan was better than no plan, right?

She explained to Sallee what would happen next: "I imagine in intricate detail what I want to create with the magic loom. Then I close my eyes and almost fall into a sort of trance. When I wake up, the thing I have imagined is real and sitting right in front of me, made out of magic Rainbow Loom elastics. I have discovered the trick is to use every drop of imagination I can muster—my imaginings need to be intricate, detailed, and as compelling as possible. Does that make any sense?"

"Not really," Sallee said with a smile. "But if it means I'm going to sleep in my own bed tonight, I support you one hundred percent."

"I have never done this with anyone watching me before," Lucy said. "I think you should close your eyes when I do. I don't want anything to mess with the magic."

Lucy pulled an envelope from the ebony box labeled *Catapult*. Lucy squeezed Sallee's hand and they both closed the eyes. Then, Lucy set to work. She pictured every specific detail of the massive machine she imagined. The magic loom hummed eagerly, channeling Lucy's vision. Lucy's hands slowly picked up speed until they tore over the loom with determination. Back and forth, over and under, the hook made the sharp, musical clicking sound Lucy loved. Lucy's heart pounded loudly as the trance took over. And then, as suddenly as it had begun, it was done.

"May I open my eyes?" Sallee asked. Lucy laughed and said yes.

In front of them was exactly the magnificent, magical contraption Lucy had envisioned—a catapult worthy of the Romans. Sallee gasped, truly impressed. Lucy reached for her friend the magic loom. She patted it and it made a low, proud rumbling sound. "Thank you," she whispered.

Lucy didn't want to waste a minute more. She whistled, calling the flock of birds from the castle wall. She quickly explained the task she needed them to do: Lucy and Sallee would climb into the small seat area and hold tightly to each other. At the same time, all together, the flock would pull back on the massive elastic lever. When Lucy shouted "Now!" the birds would let go. With just a little luck, Lucy and Sallee would catapult over the forest and the river. They would land safely back where Lucy had begun the afternoon.

"Are we ready?" Lucy shouted. Sallee hugged her close in response, the birds chirped nervously, and the magic loom glowed under her arm where she had tucked it safely. "Ok. Let's do this. One, two, three . . . Now!" With a loud, hard *snap*, the magic loom catapult shot the girls high into the sky. Together they were flung wildly through the clouds, past the dark forest, and over the river. They landed with a big bump right in front of the old fir tree.

The door was open.

❀ ❀ ❀

"Come quickly, girls—I have been waiting for you two forever," said an impatient voice. "I think I've placed everything back in the correct order on the bookshelf, but we need to move quickly here." There was Mrs. Gloucester, poking her head out from the doorway in the tree. "I've left Mr. Poppins upstairs in the Stillwater-Smith library and I don't want Abigail to find him when she wakes up."

Lucy was astonished. She couldn't believe she was actually seeing Mrs. Gloucester in the doorway, but she knew better than to spend time worrying about it. Sometimes you simply needed to trust what you saw in front of your eyes. Sallee was sitting in an awkward jumble on the ground. Lucy leaned over and gave her a hand up. "Let's go, Sallee," she said happily. "I think we are heading home."

All the while Mrs. Gloucester was tossing a mix of instructions and random thoughts in their general direction. "I think I've managed to jam both portals open, but I am not entirely sure. In any case, I need you two to close your eyes and think seriously about where you want to go. Do you have the magic loom, Lucy? Make sure you have it! We can't afford for it to go missing again."

"Yes, I've got it safe. No worries," Lucy reported back.

"Now say goodbye to each other, young ladies. If this works, you won't be seeing each other again anytime soon."

"Wait," shouted Lucy. "One more minute, please; I need one more minute." She pulled the exquisite magic loom ring off her finger and handed it to Sallee. "This is for you. If you are ever in the twenty-first century, please come and visit. You have a friend there."

"I would like that very much." Sallee began to sniffle. Lucy sensed she was trying with all her might not to cry full out. Worried an ocean of tears would spoil the magic, Lucy shouted for Mrs. Gloucester to begin. The old lady took her cue without hesitation. She leaned over the heads of the two girls and slammed the door of the fir tree shut.

Chapter Eleven

"Are you awake, Lucy?"

Lucy blinked her eyes open slowly, ever so happy to hear Dr. Smith's voice.

"Is Dad with you, Mum?"

"Yes, I'm here, peaches. I hear you had an interesting day."

"Yes, Dad, it was a very interesting day. I'm so sorry, Mum. Are you still mad at me?"

"I couldn't stay mad at you for more than an hour, Lucy. Now go to sleep. We'll talk in the morning."

"One more thing, Mum—Mrs. Gloucester brought Mr. Poppins by to play this afternoon and she picked up the package. Turns out it was hers all along. Oh, and I left a letter on the kitchen table for Alyssa. Will you mail it for me in the morning?"

"Of course, my beautiful girl. Now go to sleep."

❋ ❋ ❋

Dear Alyssa,
You won't believe all that has happened since this morning. I miss you right now more than I ever have since the day you left. Really. That's 100% true and no lie. I HAVE SO MUCH TO TELL YOU. But it's all a secret. I can't send the news by text or tell you over the phone. Write me back at once and promise me you won't tell anyone anything NO MATTER WHAT. If you do, I will write at once and tell you EVERYTHING! Promise.
All my love,
Your true best friend forever,
Lucy Stillwater-Smith

A sneak peak of Lucy's
next adventure,

*Lucy and the Magic Loom:
The Daring Rescue*

Chapter One

Lucy Stillwater-Smith was sitting on her bed, puffy-eyed and sniffling. Her very best friend, Alyssa, had moved to America just one year ago and was visiting Lucy for the summer. But today was the day Lucy had been dreading, when Alyssa would fly back across the wide Atlantic Ocean to New York City. Lucy knew that the old white stone town house at 163 Terrier Square would not be the same.

The door creaked open. Lucy looked up and saw two big brown eyes and a splash of gold hair peering at her through the crack in the door. "Alyssa?" Alyssa came into the room and flung her arms around Lucy. The two girls had spent the summer visiting all of Alyssa's favorite spots in London; one night they got dressed up and went to a fancy musical, and they took day trips to hilly parts of the countryside. They gorged on their favorite snacks, like curry chips and chocolate biscuits, and every night they stayed up late, giggling under an elaborate fort made of sheets in Lucy's bedroom.

"I'm going to miss you, too!" Alyssa said before Lucy could try to explain her puffy eyes. They hugged each other tightly, and suddenly Lucy felt a pinch on her head.

"Ouch! Your bracelet is stuck in my hair!" They had made each other elastic friendship bracelets, which were the best and by far the most beautiful of any they had ever seen. But they could get caught on things. Very carefully, Alyssa unhooked the bracelet's plastic clasp and removed it from the tangles in Lucy's brown hair.

Alyssa fiddled with the clasp to get the friendship bracelet back on her wrist. "Just make a knot, it'll be faster," said Lucy. She tied a knot and the two girls put their bracelets next to each other and smiled. "You can *never* take yours off, got it?"

Alyssa's eyes widened. "Like that would ever happen! Every day we'll look at our wrists and know the other person is looking too, and we'll be friends forever."

"Knock, knock, ladies—incoming!" Miss Abigail Sanders bustled into the bedroom and dropped a pile of clean laundry onto the bed. "Oh, you darlings," Abigail said with a frown when she noticed the pile of tissues that Lucy had collected on her bed. "I know you're going to miss each other, but just think of all the fun you've had this summer!"

"I don't want Alyssa to go, Abigail! It's not fair—can't she stay?"

"Can't I? Can't I stay?" Alyssa chimed in.

Abigail's eyes twinkled. "I think Alyssa's parents might have something to say about that. How about some tea and biscuits before you get ready for your flight? Will that help?" The girls' moods instantly shifted and they nodded approvingly. Abigail always knew how to make everything better. She had taken care of Lucy for Lucy's whole life, and while Lucy could now do basically everything on her own, Abigail was still wonderful for all of the little things, like knowing which snacks to buy, and big things, too, like making sure the Doctors didn't forget to go to Lucy's recitals.

"The Doctors" were Lucy's parents. Dr. Stillwater was her dad. He researched cures for all kinds of infectious diseases, with a particular emphasis on the gross ones. Dr. Smith was her mum, and she worked in a hospital that helped children who had cancer. Lucy loved them both to the moon and back, but they were also very important people with very important jobs, which meant that Lucy didn't get to see them all that often.

Abigail floated out of the room and her voice carried from the hallway as she said she'd start the teakettle. Lucy jumped off the bed and hopped over Alyssa's nearly full suitcase toward the door. "Are you coming, Alyssa?" Alyssa's eyes were caught on something on the bookshelf, and she murmured distractedly about needing to put a couple more things in her suitcase. "Okay, whatever, I'll be downstairs but just hurry up!"

Lucy pranced around the kitchen, excited for tea and biscuits. Abigail had put out a plate already, and Lucy was getting antsy waiting for Alyssa. After several minutes, the teakettle shrieked and Lucy realized that Alyssa was still not downstairs.

"*ALYSSAAAAA!*" She went to the bottom of the stairs. "Come on—this is your last opportunity for English tea! American tea is just *terrible!*" She waited to hear a giggle from Alyssa, but there was no response.

Lucy started up the stairs. "Alyssa? We can finish packing later." Lucy pushed open her bedroom door but there was no one there. She checked every room on the floor, all of which were empty. She took a seat on her bed, checking her phone to see if Alyssa had texted her. Maybe this was a joke.

In the corner of her room, something caught her eye. Alyssa's friendship bracelet lay undone on the floor, right next to the spot where Lucy kept her magic loom secretly stowed away. She studied the bracelet, then knelt down beside the bookshelf and scoured through its contents. A year ago, Lucy had received a magical Rainbow Loom in the mail, one that brought her to another world of magical creatures. She had used her Rainbow Loom skills to make her way through the world and help a new friend. But as she searched her shelf, the magic loom was gone, and so was her best friend.